# OLIVIA™
## Meets Olivia

adapted by Ellie O'Ryan

based on the screenplay "The Two Olivias" written by Pat Resnick

illustrated by Art Mawhinney and Shane L. Johnson

Simon Spotlight

New York  London  Toronto  Sydney  New Delhi

Based on the TV series *OLIVIA*™ as seen on Nickelodeon™

SIMON SPOTLIGHT
An imprint of Simon & Schuster Children's Publishing Division
1230 Avenue of the Americas, New York, New York 10020
For information about special discounts for bulk purchases, please contact Simon & Schuster
Special Sales at 1-866-506-1949 or business@simonandschuster.com.
Manufactured in the United States of America   0312 LAK
2 3 4 5 6 7 8 9 10
ISBN 978-1-4424-4707-3

*Ring! Ring! Ring!*
Mrs. Hoggenmuller rang her cowbell three times, like she did every morning.

Olivia sat up very straight, like she did every morning. School was about to start, and Olivia, like always, was ready!

Mrs. Hoggenmuller stood at the front of the class. A new classmate stood next to her. "Good morning, children," Mrs. Hoggenmuller said. "We have a new student joining our class today."

A new student! Olivia was so excited! "Can the new girl sit next to me?" she asked.

"That would be very nice, Olivia, because you two have a lot in common," Mrs. Hoggenmuller said. "In fact there's something about you that is absolutely identical. Olivia, meet Olivia!"

Olivia's smile disappeared. "But *my* name is Olivia!" she said.

"You're *both* named Olivia," replied Mrs. Hoggenmuller, turning to face the chalkboard. "Now it's time for math. Who knows what four plus two is?" Both Olivias waved their hands in the air.

"Yes, Olivia," Mrs. Hoggenmuller said. But *which* Olivia did she mean?

"She was looking at *me*," Olivia said.

"But she pointed at *me*," the new Olivia said.

"From now on, Olivia will be Olivia One, and our new Olivia will be Olivia Two," Mrs. Hoggenmuller decided.

Olivia couldn't believe it. She had a new girl in her class, a new desk mate, and a new nickname—and it wasn't even lunchtime yet!

After school Olivia had lots of questions. So she found someone who had lots of answers—her dad.

"How can there be anyone else named Olivia?" she asked. "It isn't fair. Her parents didn't ask if they could use my name!"

Olivia's dad smiled. "But it's a good thing! It means a lot of people like the name. Every year more people name their babies Olivia. Maybe one day *everybody* will be named Olivia!" he joked.

Olivia imagined sitting in the kitchen with her family . . .

   "*Please pass the salt, Olivia,*" *Mom says to Dad.*

   "*This is a really good dinner, Olivia,*" *Ian says to Mom.*

   *Ding! Dong! goes the doorbell.*

   "*Package for Olivia!*" *calls the mailman.*

   "*That's me!*" *the entire family replies.*

. . . Olivia shuddered. It would be *terrible* if everyone were named Olivia!

The next day at school, the confusion over the two Olivias continued. "Your turn, Olivia," called Daisy from the slide. But she was talking to the *other* Olivia.

"I'm having a playdate with Olivia!" Francine exclaimed. But she was talking about the *other* Olivia.

When Mrs. Hoggenmuller passed back the class art projects, she accidentally switched the two Olivias' projects.

"You got mine by mistake," Olivia said.

"I like yours better," Olivia Two said. "Let's trade!"

"But I'd like to take my drawing home," Olivia protested.

"Hey! Don't be mean to Olivia Two, Olivia One!" Francine said.

Olivia sighed. Two Olivias in the same class just wasn't going to work.

That afternoon Olivia made a big announcement. "Mom," she said, "I've decided something important. I'm changing my name to Pam!"

"Why would you do that?" asked her mom.

"Because I don't know any other Pams," explained Olivia. "I'd be the only one."

"Well, if you want to call yourself Pam, you can," Mom said.

"Okay!" Olivia exclaimed. "Pam it is."

Pam told *everyone* at school about her new name—her friends,
Mrs. Hoggenmuller, and even Olivia Two.
"Who knows how many days there are in the week?" Mrs. Hoggenmuller
asked. "Olivia?"
Pam and Olivia Two answered at the same time.
"Olivia Two gets a gold star!" Mrs. Hoggenmuller said.
"But I had my hand up first!" said Pam.
"She called on Olivia," Olivia Two said. "*Your* name is Pam."

During recess Pam did a lot of thinking. "I don't know if Pam is the right name for me," she said to Julian.

"You don't want to be called Pam anymore?" asked Julian.

"I just don't feel very Pam-ish. But I always feel Olivia-ish!" she replied.

"Definitely," agreed Julian. "You're definitely Olivia-ish!"

Olivia was very happy to be Olivia once more. After school she rushed up to her mom. "I decided to be an Olivia again!" she announced.

"I'm so glad," Olivia's mom replied. "All Olivias are special, but you're an especially special Olivia to me."

Olivia knew she had made the right decision to change her name back to Olivia.

But there was still the problem of the *other* Olivia.

What was she going to do?

Olivia imagined that she was in the Wild West, wearing a cowboy hat and a sheriff's badge . . .

"This here town just isn't big enough for two Olivias," Olivia says.

"Yeah?" asks Olivia Two. "What are you going to do about it?"

"We're going to have a duel," Olivia replies. "Whoever loses the duel clears out of town."

Each Olivia throws her ball high in the air—and catches it! Then they throw their balls even higher. Olivia Two reaches and reaches—and just barely catches her ball!

Olivia runs in circles, her arm outstretched. The ball lands in her glove. But then it bounces out!

Olivia dives through the dirt and catches the ball just before it hits the ground!

"That was some catch!" Olivia Two says. She is very impressed.

"Your catch was pretty good, too," Olivia replies. "Let's call it a tie. From now on, this is a two-Olivia town!"

Olivia's daydream gave her an idea. Maybe there was room for two Olivias at school after all. Maybe they could even be friends! During recess she walked up to Olivia Two. "So how do you like our school, Olivia Two?" she asked.

"It's pretty good," Olivia Two replied.

"I'm glad you like it," Olivia said. She gave Olivia Two a big smile.

And Olivia Two smiled back!

"I'll give you back your painting, if you want it," Olivia Two said shyly.

"Thanks! I was thinking that maybe we should start an Olivia club, just for *Olivias*," replied Olivia.

"That sounds great!" said Olivia Two.

After school the two Olivias made a clubhouse for the Olivia Club.

"What should we do now?" asked Olivia Two.

Just then Ian poked his head in the clubhouse. "Hi! Can I come in?"
he asked.

Olivia shook her head. "No, this is a club for Olivias only," she said.

The two Olivias tried to think of something to do. Olivia didn't want to play
checkers. And Olivia Two didn't want to sing a song or play hide-and-seek.

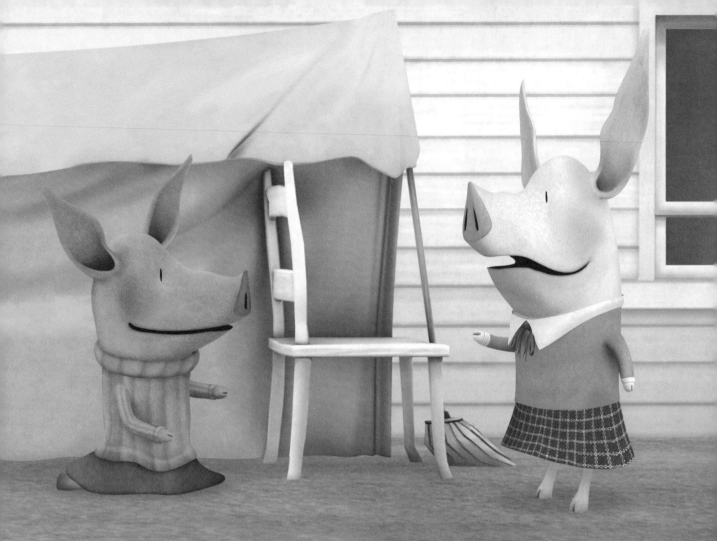

"Hi!" called Francine. "Can I play?"

"No Francines allowed," Olivia Two said, sadly. "Only Olivias."

The two Olivias looked at each other as they realized that all they had in common was the name Olivia.

"A club with just Olivias isn't very fun after all," Olivia One said.

The two Olivias agreed! So they ran off to play tag with Ian and Francine.

At bedtime Olivia had one more question for her dad. "Why do you think a bed is called a bed?" she asked.

"It's just a word that someone made up," Dad explained.

"Like Olivia is a word meaning me?" Olivia asked.

"That's right," Dad said. "Good night, Olivia."